Story drawing book

To Mia and Delilah

Published in 2021 by Story Drawing Club.

Supported by Arts Council England.

First edition, published by Story Drawing Club

ISBN: 978-1-3999-0710-1

A catalogue record of this book is available from the British Library.

October 2021

Printed by Mixam, Hertfordshire, UK

My name is...

— — — — — — — — — — — — —

— — — — — — — — — — — —

(A brand new member of the Story Drawing Club!)

HOW TO USE THIS BOOK

Hi!

HELLO!

We're Story Drawing Club!

If you want to learn how to draw and write your own stories then this book makes you our newest member! We're going to show you how to draw characters based on yourself, your friends and your family - so you can make yourself the star of your very own story!

Not sure how to use this book? Here are our top tips...

Don't worry about making mistakes. It doesn't have to be perfect to be good.

Don't give up! You are good at drawing and writing. Don't let yourself be told otherwise.

Everyone can draw and tell stories - you just practise to get better.

Have fun!

YOU WILL NEED THE MIGHTY PENCIL!

You can fill out this whole book using the humble (but amazing) pencil!

Look on the next page to find out what else might be useful for this book.

ALSO USEFUL

pencil crayons

sharpener

paint brush

charcoal

eraser

scissors

PVA glue

paint

yellow ochre

MARK MAKING

Learning to make different marks is an important part of drawing.

Mark making gives texture and movement to your drawings, and is really useful for drawing different hair types (which you'll work on in a few pages). You can use pencils and pens as well as charcoal or paint - be inspired!

Here are some examples of marks made with a 4B pencil. By pressing lightly or heavily on the paper, and by drawing different patterns you can create lots of different marks! Now, grab a pencil, choose your favourite marks and see if you can recreate them in the boxes opposite!

You can also have a go at making up your own marks and patterns!

DRAWING FEATURES

When you're drawing a portrait try to look for the shapes in the features of the face. For example, when you look at an eye, the outside shape looks like an oval – almost lemon shaped! Have a look at your own eyes in the mirror. Can you see the different shapes?

lemon

Use the space below to a have a go at drawing an eye, you can use the example to help you with your drawing. Look at the shape of the eyebrow too and see if you can draw it above the eye.

The iris is a circle. The pupil is almost a circle, but part of it is hidden by the eyelid. You can add eyelashes too if you want!

The nose can be drawn in different ways. The simplest way is to look for the shape at the bottom of the nose where the nostrils are. Have a go at copying the noses below, and look at your own nose in the mirror for reference. Try to look at the ear as a series of shapes too.

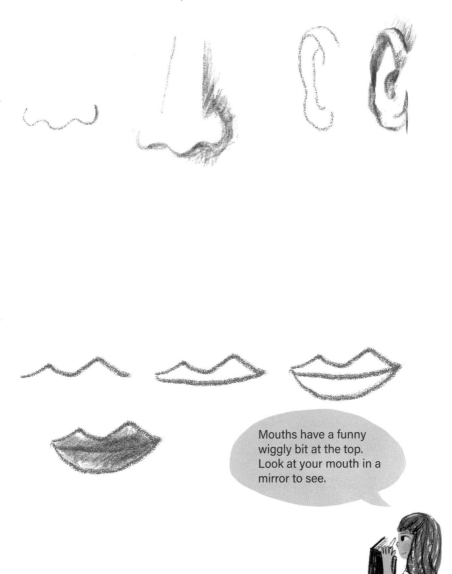

Mouths have a funny wiggly bit at the top. Look at your mouth in a mirror to see.

PORTRAITS

If I want to draw a character for a story, I start by drawing a portrait of someone I know. It stops me from drawing the same sort of character!

1. Draw an oval shape

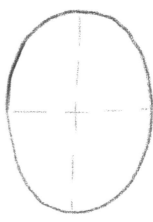

2. Draw faint lines across and down the centre of the oval

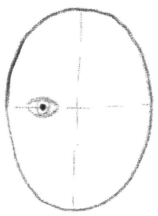

3. Start by drawing one eye first and then draw the 2nd

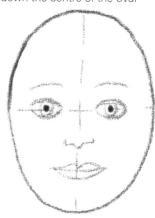

4. Draw in the nose, mouth and eyebrows

Use the steps on the opposite page to draw a portrait of yourself or someone else and use your new mark making skills to draw the hair. If you can see the ears, draw them too.

Look in a mirror to draw yourself. Or draw someone else, (if they will stay still long enough!)

Extra drawing
space!

CHARACTERS

Now you have your portrait to base a new character on!

So let's practise drawing different expressions and hairstyles on characters, and work out how to get the skin tone right. Then when you've practised these elements, you're going to create a character using the portrait you drew earlier to help prompt you.

You can draw a main character who looks like you!

Or me!

EXPRESSIONS

Experiment with different expressions for your character. Expressions bring your character to life by telling us how they're feeling. Which eyes and mouths would suit certain emotions, such as feeling happy, angry, tired or excited? And which is the right nose for your character? Try some out on the opposite page...

EYES

NOSES

Now you have a go!

MOUTHS

My tip is that eyebrows slanting up can mean surprise and down can mean anger or unhappiness.

HAIRSTYLES

Have a go at creating the characters below. You can learn how to use different marks to create different hair types, or headwear so you can draw yourself or your family or your friends easily. These are the styles people ask for help with the most, but there are more examples on the following pages.

Layer up the suggested lines or marks over each other to create the final effect.

HAIR AND EXPRESSIONS

Now you've had a practice, bring your hairstyles and expressions together to invent new characters! You can even put names under them and how they're feeling.

thanks!

SKIN TONE

Everyone has different skin tone, so it is important to get it right when you are trying to get the character to look like yourself or someone else. Pencil can be used to create darker and lighter shades, perfect for different skin tones!

PENCIL

1. With your pencil make the lightest mark you can while scribbling.

2. Press a little harder on the paper as you scribble to make a slightly darker tone.

3. Gradually apply more pressure on your pencil to increase the darkness of the pencil mark, depending on how dark the skin tone of your character is.

Now you have a go!

PENCIL CRAYONS

Some shops sell crayons especially for skin tone. But if you don't have these, you can use a combination of the colours **orange**, **brown**, **pink**, **beige** and **yellow**. Layer up the colours for different skin tones - have a go at the following combinations below or experiment with your own!

Use this space to have a go.

25

WATERCOLOUR

If you have watercolour paints, they are also good for skin tone. The more or less water you add the lighter or darker the tone. You can also mix colours to match your skin tone, use the space below to have a go.

MATCH YOUR SKIN TONE

Use this page to try out pencils, crayons, paints or all three to match your skin colour.

Don't worry if it goes the wrong colour first time. You can just try again!

CHARACTERS

So you've had the chance to practise the different elements that make up a character. Now make a whole character based on your wonderful portrait from earlier. This character is going to look like YOU or the person you've drawn, and will be the main character of the story that you write later on in this book.

Draw a rough oval on top of a rectangle.

Next, draw two lines for the arms and hands at the end.

Now, draw the legs using rough rectangle shapes.

Finally, draw the feet.

Now you have a go!

After you've drawn the body, add your features, skin tone and clothes to your character!

1.

Draw a rough oval on top of a rectangle.

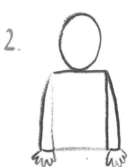

2.

Next draw two lines for the arms and hands at the end.

3.

Now draw the legs using rough oval shapes.

4.

Finally, draw in the wheels, back and supports on the chair.

Now you have a go!

[y]ou don't know what [clot]hes to draw, take [insp]iration from what you [are] wearing right now!

Here's some extra space to practise your characters!

STICK FIGURES

As you get more confident and want to introduce actions, stick figures are great for working out the pose or action for characters. Then you can draw their real bodies over the top, like in these examples...

Can you draw your character jumping, hopping, doing a wheelie or anything you want!?

WRITING YOUR STORY

Now you have a main character for your story! Over the next few pages you're going to get everything you need to tell your tale.

But before we start, here are a few tips...

1. It's okay to be fantastical: big ideas are beautiful!

2. Stories aren't all about writing. A picture speaks a thousand words.

3. Write about things from your own life - it's what you know best. That means your own home, school, friends and family.

4. Storytellers care much more about interesting characters and exciting plots than their spelling and grammar.

I'm dyslexic but it doesn't stop me having great story ideas!

Ready to write a story then?

START WITH A GOOD STORY

One tip for writing good stories is to take a great story and make it your own. We're going to use Little Red Riding Hood. What elements make it a great story?

MAIN CHARACTER

Red Riding Hood obviously. She's the hero.

SPECIAL OBJECT

She has a stylish cape – it's pretty special.

THE MISSION

She has a mission. She has to go to see her gran.

THE ANIMAL

Howdy

The wolf! The Big Bad Wolf!

CHOOSE YOUR ANIMAL

Your story is going to have an animal in it too! Use the sections below to write some details about the animal character in your story.

Does your animal have a name?

_____

_____

_____

Choose an animal from the page opposite - either draw it or cut it out and stick here.

Is your animal cheeky, funny, serious?

_____

_____

_____

Draw your animal!

animal is a windy unicorn
misses his friend.

Ahhh, cute.
And smelly.

What is your object and why is it special?

CHOOSE YOUR OBJECT

Use the sections below to write some details about your object.

What does your object do that is special? Is it magic?

_____

_____

_____

Choose an object from the page opposite - either draw it or cut it out and stick here.

What adventure will you go on with your object?

_____

_____

_____

41

YOU VS.

Write your Superhero name here. (Tip: 'Super" + your name?)

Turn yourself into your story's main character by answering the following questions.

 1 What are you best at?
(e.g. picking your nose)

 2 Now turn it into a superpower
(you can flick your bogies
hundreds of metres!?)

3 What's your secret mission?
(Think of something you or
your character really wants)

4 Where does it take you to?
(Think of somewhere you'd
love to go!)

42

YOUR ANIMAL

- - - - - - - - - - - - -

(Write your animal's name here, like The Big, Bad Wolf)

Imagine more about your animal's character too.

1 Bad habit
(For Red Riding Hood's wolf,
this was eating grandmas!)

_____

_____

2 Weakness
(After dinner naps, Mr Wolf?)

_____

_____

3 Where do they live?

_____

4 Why do they try to stop your character?

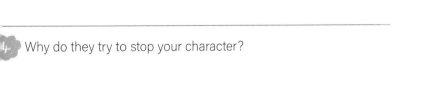

_____

_____

STORY FRAME GAME

Now you have your character, your mission, your special object and your animal, you can use the story frame of Little Red Riding Hood to create your own story. Where there are blanks, change the details to your story. Soon it will be unrecognisable!

Is it copying though?

Not really! Most stories have similar things in them: a hero with a quest, someone trying to stop them, a special object. It's your ideas that make it special and interesting.

Little Red Riding Hood had a special cape

and went on a mission to take food to her Grandma.

He/she/they went for a walk and met a wolf

who wanted to eat her up.

So it dressed up in her Grandma's clothes

and tricked her into being his dinner.

But fortunately a lumberjack came and rescued them.

To celebrate Little Red went for tea and scones with her Grandma.

Now you have a go!

RULES OF THE GAME:
Change as many details
of the story as you can!

You'll make a
completely new story!

_____ had a _____

and went on a mission to _____

He/she/they _____ and met a _____

who wanted _____

So it _____

and _____

But fortunately _____

To celebrate _____

_____

45

Now you have everything you need to write your story in full, you can use these next few pages to write it out in as much detail as you want!

Story title:

_____

One day...

_____

_____

_____

_____

_____

_____

_____

_____

_____

_____

_____

_____

_____

_____

_____

_____

_____

_____

_____

_____

_____

_____

Well done, you've finished your story! Now go back
and give your story a name (if you haven't already).

SCENES

Now that you have your story you need to paint or draw the scenes that will help to bring your story to life! Look at how picture books help to bring excitement and interest to stories, through the drawing and painting of fun characters and vivid backgrounds!

Think about which characters are in the scene and what they're doing.

Choose a section from your story that you want to draw or paint.

Where is it set? Inside or outside? In your bedroom or in another country?

What's happening in the scene?

THUMBNAIL SKETCHES

A thumbnail sketch is a little drawing where you can try out your ideas and composition first before you commit more time and energy to a larger drawing or painting. Below are some thumbnail sketches of Red Riding Hood, but how could you do the same with your story?

Little Red went into the woods

hellooo

She met a very friendly wolf!

Your thumbnail sketches really don't have to be perfect, in fact they can be quite rough!

Think of a scene that you would like to draw and have a go at your own thumbnail sketches here - have as many goes as you want, either with the same sentence or different sentences.

1.

2.

Choose a sentence from your story and write it at the bottom, like in the example.

3.

4.

Give your ideas space!

Use this page to practise more thumbnail sketches, if you want to!

CREATING SCENES

Once you have drawn your thumbnail sketches for your scenes, it's time to paint or draw large versions of your scenes with more detail.

Scenes can be created using any type of medium that you have to hand, using pattern and shading to create interest and detail. Or you could use collage, paint or printing. The next few pages will show you different techniques to help you create your scenes and illustrate your story.

PENCIL PATTERNS

If you don't have crayons or paints nearby, you can still create an amazing scene using pencil alone, just by adding patterns and shading. Remember your mark making techniques that you used at the beginning of this book?

Have a go at drawing the drawers or the plant either copying them as they are or adding your own patterns.

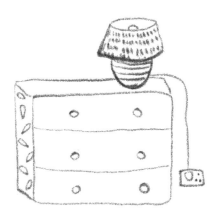

55

COLLAGE

Add colour and texture to your picture by using a technique called collage. Grab your scissors and some newspaper, magazines or tissue paper to cut up!

Always check first before you cut up someone's favourite magazine! And definitely don't cut up anyone's book...

Use this space to experiment with some collage - can you create your own plant or something else using this technique?

MAKE YOUR OWN PAINT

If you haven't got paint at home, you can make your own!
Just follow the recipe below.

Ingredients
    1/2 cup of salt
    1/2 cup of hot water
    1/2 cup of flour
    Food colouring

Recipe
1. In a large bowl mix together the water and salt until as much of the salt has dissolved which will help to give the paint a smoother texture.
2. Stir in the flour.
3. Divide into separate containers and mix in your chosen food colouring.

Tip
Not got food colouring?
Dry spices can give great colour.
Try chili powder or paprika
for red, turmeric for orange
and curry powder for yellow.

You can even make your own paint brushes, out of leaves, or sponges tied to sticks. See what you can find and make!

tie with string

PRINTING

Printing is a lovely technique that can be used in your illustrations. You can use fruit or vegetables: chop a potato in half and see if an adult can help you to cut a shape in it, then dip it in paint to print with. Or a thumb print, or a leaf! See what you can find that might create an interesting print.

Go to www.storydrawingclub.com to find some free printing inspiration!

Now you have a go!

You could also try printing with toilet roll ends, a rubber, or bottle tops.

SPEECH BUBBLES

Your characters can also express themselves in speech bubbles just like this in every drawing you do. You can make them say whatever you want them to! It's another way to tell your story with words and images.

SILLY

WOW! A MERMAID

Hellooooooo!

SCARED

HEEEEELP! IT WANTS TO EEEAT MEEE!

Q: How would your character respond to a talking seal?
A: It depends on who they are and how they feel...

CURIOUS

HI! CAN YOU BREATHE UNDERWATER

Now you have a go!

Grab a pencil and practise writing in these speech bubbles!

Scene 1.

Challenge:
Go back to your thumbnail sketches and use the next few pages to create full coloured or detailed scenes. Draw your characters into a scene and think about what will be in the background? How can you bring it to life using pattern, colour, collage?

write your sentence here ↘

Scene 2.

Use a mix of media in your scene - for example you might use pencil and collage together! Using a mix of media can help give your scene even more impact!

Scene 3.

Scene 4.

Extra drawing space!

So you have come to the end of the Story Drawing Book!

Congratulations! Now you know how to write and illustrate your own story, you can carry on with the one you have started in this book and complete it - and send it to a publisher!

This book is just a starting point for writing and drawing! Don't let your stories stop when you have filled up all the pages. You can write and draw in a notebook, on paper, an old envelope – whatever you can get your hands on that will help you get your fantastic ideas out into the world!

Story Drawing club x

WHAT NEXT?

Want some ideas for what to do next?
Aim to complete four finished scenes that are full of characters, detail, colour, and a completed story.

Get a sketchbook!
Sketchbooks are a great place to keep drawing, writing and experimenting with ideas. They don't have to cost a lot – you could ask for one for your birthday!

Make your own mini book
See if you can write and illustrate your own mini book. You can make your own mini book by folding one piece of paper!

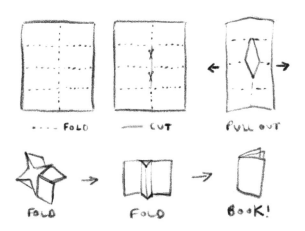

See a video of instructions of how to make a mini book at
www.storydrawingclub.com

Look at the work by lots of different artists!
It can be so inspiring to look at artists' work to help motivate you to try new things. See the artists on the next page to get started.

INSPIRING ARTISTS

Some of our favourite artists and authors for you to look up...

Amazing and incredibly prolific illustrator and author, creating lots of beautiful picture books in a very short time! *Look Up* is our favourite - look it up!

Dapo Adeola

Beatrice creates beautiful scenes for her picture books, full of different textures and wonky lines to create wonderful and sometimes quite surre story worlds...

Beatrice Alemagne

Brilliant illustrator and author, creating touching and funny picture books including *Stuck*, where a boy throws everything up into a tree to get down his kite.

Oliver Jeffers

Nadia's a wonderfu illustrator and autho whose debut book *Good Little Wolf* is one of our favourite with its beautiful illustrations and witty storyline.

Nadia Shireen

Amazing New York artist who went from an unknown grafitti artist to highly paid gallery artist. His vibrant paintings inspire us to be bold with our drawing!

Jean-Michel Basquiat

An absolutely awesome artist who painted gigantic murals in public spaces so that his a could be accessible everyone.

Keith Haring

A groundbreaking Mexican painter who painted using striking colours and focused on portraits, self–portraits, animals (especially monkeys!) and the natural world.

Frida Kahlo

Turner Prize winner fantastic painter, loo out for Lubaina's life size cut-out portrait that really make an impact.

Lubaina Himid

BEING CREATIVE IS NOT JUST FOR ARTISTS

Want to become a leading scientist? Being creative can help you think outside the box, and think of new ideas!

Did you know drawing improves reading and writing? Crack out the pencil and paper!

Did you know, many scientists who have received prestigious honors such as the Nobel Prize are also artists?

Do you enjoy crafting, making and stitching? These skills are integral for surgeons, where a steady hand and good stitching skills are vital for life saving operations.

Want to be a vet? Drawing trains you to look more closely at objects, giving you better observational skills. This might help you see if something is wrong with animals when giving them a check up.

Feeling stressed out or unhappy? Drawing or writing something helps you to express yourself and can be very calming. So whatever you do, keep creating to help stay happy!

INDEX OF USEFUL WORDS

Media - in the context of creating art, media refers to materials and tools used by an artist to create their work (i.e. paintbrush and paint).

Mixed media - when an artist uses a mix of media to create a piece of artwork (i.e. paint, charcoal, and crayons could be used in one painting).

Canvas - fabric that painters use to paint on.

Texture - in art refers to the surface quality of a painting, i.e. does the paint add texture on the page or is it smooth?

Illustration - drawing or painting that works as a visual explanation of a text, concept or process.

Expressions - facial expressions are a form of non verbal communication.

Features - facial features include the eyes, ears, nose, mouth, eyebrows and hair.

Mark making - a term used for the creation of different patterns, lines, textures and shapes. This may be on a piece of paper, on the floor, outside in the garden or on an object or surface.

Proportion - the size of an object in relation to other objects. When drawing scenes, proportion shows closer things as bigger and distant things as smaller.

Composition - the placement of your characters and background objects together to produce an overall effect for your scenes.

Turner Prize - named after the English painter J. M. W. Turner, is a yearly arts prize awarded to a British artist or group of artists.

BIG THANKS

To The Arts Council, England for funding this book project and the development of Story Drawing Club!

To Andria Zafirakou and George Streets at AiR, London for their ongoing advice and support, and helping to take Story Drawing Club to so many schools!

To Z-arts, Manchester for their mentoring and support.

To the children at Manley Park Primary School for their invaluable feedback.

To all the Story Drawing Club children we've worked with in schools over the years.

To Rania Hafez for setting Emma off on this journey several years ago.

To Mia and Delilah for all the drawing and feedback that has helped Story Drawing Club grow over the past 5 years!

ABOUT THE AUTHORS

Emma Jackson and **David Jackson** run Story Drawing Club workshops in schools in Manchester, London and Sheffield.

Emma is an illustrator and workshop leader. During her MA in Illustration at Sheffield Hallam University, Emma developed the Story Drawing Club project to give more children of all backgrounds inspiring artistic experiences.

David is a writer and academic at Manchester Metropolitan University with a PhD in storywriting games.